LEGO EXO-FORCE

ESCAPE FROM SENTAI MOUNTAIN

LEGO EXO-FORCE™

ESCAPE FROM SENTAI MOUNTAIN

BY GREG FARSHTEY

SCHOLASTIC INC.

New York   Toronto   London   Auckland   Sydney
Mexico City   New Delhi   Hong Kong   Buenos Aires

ISBN 0-439-82808-2

12 11 10 9 8 7 6 5 4 3 2 1   6 7 8 9 10 11/0

Printed in the U.S.A.
First printing, September 2006

CHAPTER 1

Hikaru soared through the sky in the Stealth Hunter as he patrolled the northern side of Sentai Mountain. The Stealth Hunter, a powerful armored battle machine, was equipped with boot jets that let it fly at top speed. It also had sensors built in so Hikaru could spot anything moving on the ground far below. From up high, he could see all of Sentai Mountain. It was a sight that made him sad. At one time, the mountain had been so beautiful. Now it was scarred by battle.

As he turned to head back to base, he thought about the past. Once, humans had lived in peace on the mountain. To help them with mining and other tasks, they had built robots. The robots could go where

humans could not, lift heavy loads, and do dangerous tasks in place of humans.

Then everything went terribly wrong. The robot miners turned evil and rebelled against the humans. Great battles took place as the robots tried to seize control of the mountain. The energies unleashed were so powerful that they split Sentai Mountain in half!

It was only with great effort that the humans were able to drive the robots away. The robots were forced all the way down to the bottom of the gorge between the two halves of the mountain. With the robots gone, peace returned to the settlements, and bridges were built to link the two sides of the mountain together again. But no one believed the danger was really over. A team

of scientists and engineers, led by a skilled inventor named Ryo, went to work building armored battle machines that the humans could use to defend themselves.

Hikaru snapped back to attention as his flight path took him into a dense cloud bank. In the early days of the battle machines, he would have been flying blind. Fortunately, improvements were made to the armored suits all the time, including high-tech sensors. Hikaru checked his sensor readouts and saw there were no obstacles in his path. He looked away from the sensor screen without noticing that it showed something approaching him from behind.

Hikaru thought again of the past. Those who had believed the humans of Sentai Mountain were still in danger were right. The robots had been defeated, but only temporarily. While at the bottom of the gorge, they repaired themselves and their battle machines and prepared to strike again.

It happened on a bright, clear summer morning. Villagers on the southern half of the mountain heard the frightening sounds of turbojet engines and clanking armor. Then the robot army appeared on the horizon. Powerful Sentries led the way, followed by the flying Fire Vultures and the massive Thunder Furies. Each was piloted by one of the robot rebels. Most humans fled and made it across the bridges to the northern side of the mountain. But some were not fast enough and were captured.

The humans scrambled to stop the robot invasion. Untrained pilots in battle machines were just barely able to defend the bridges, but they were not skilled enough to drive the robots off the southern side of the mountain. In a matter of hours, the robots had claimed half the mountain, and many villagers had become their prisoners.

It was a disaster. Worse, everyone knew the robots were not going to stop their attacks. Eventually, they would capture the northern side of the mountain, too. The humans' only hope was to form a specially trained team of battle machine pilots to guard the northern side of the mountain.

And so the EXO-FORCE team was born. Young men and women from all over the villages volunteered to become battle machine pilots. The training was long and hard since there were always new weapons

or instruments a pilot had to learn to use. When their training was done, the pilots were assigned to battle machines based on their skill levels. Hikaru was one of the best pilots on the team, so he got to fly the sleek, fast, and powerful Stealth Hunter.

Right now, Hikaru was making the Stealth Hunter dive out of the clouds and head for home base. But his trip was about to be interrupted. A jet of flame shot past his cockpit — so close he could feel the heat even through the battle machine's armor. He didn't need to check his sensors to know who had fired it at him. A Fire Vulture was closing in to attack!

Hikaru triggered his turbo boost to put some distance between himself and the flying robot battle machine. He had to get out of range of the Fire Vulture's flamethrower before turning to counterattack. Although the Stealth Hunter was

a little faster than the enemy, it was not as heavily armored. Speed and skill were the only way to beat the Fire Vulture.

The Stealth Hunter shot forward and then straight up to gain altitude, spinning as it did so. Now Hikaru could see that there was only one Fire Vulture after him. It was piloted by a silver Devastator robot. Attacks by several Fire Vultures on the bridges happened a lot—it was strange to see one operating by itself this close to the EXO-FORCE team's headquarters.

"Well, I'll teach that bucket of bolts not to wander," Hikaru said to himself as he powered up his laser rifle. He took aim at the Fire Vulture's left arm—its most vulnerable spots since the "body" of the  machine was heavily armored to protect the pilot.

Before he could shoot, the Fire Vulture suddenly veered left, dove, spun, and came up underneath the Stealth Hunter. A sudden burst of flame from its weapon damaged the Stealth Hunter's left boot jet. The right jet was still working, but with no thrust from the left one to provide balance, the Stealth Hunter toppled in the sky and shot toward the ground.

Don't panic, Hikaru thought. *Remember*

what Sensei Keiken taught you. There's always a way to win. I just have to find it.

Just because one boot jet was out of action, it didn't mean the Stealth Hunter was helpless in a fight. Hikaru dove into a cloud and then engaged full stealth mode. The battle machine was now invisible to enemy sensors and even the heat from its thrusters was masked. There was no way for the Fire Vulture to locate the Stealth Hunter using its sensors. If it wanted to find the Stealth Hunter, it would have to search inside the cloud bank. This would make it an easy target for Hikaru.

While hidden in the clouds, Hikaru picked up bursts of static over his communication link. That could only be the robot pilot sending a transmission, calling for reinforcements. Damaged as his battle machine was, Hikaru could not hope to fight off a whole group of Fire Vultures.

But maybe I can get them to head somewhere else, he thought.

The Stealth Hunter hovered in the cloud bank and waited. The sensors showed the Fire Vulture circling just outside, not sure if its target was in the clouds. Hikaru forced himself to be calm. He would get one chance to make his plan work and he had to be ready when it came.

The robot pilot made a decision. It wasn't going to wait for help. Instead, it steered the Fire Vulture into the cloud. This was what Hikaru had been hoping for.

Hikaru spotted the Fire Vulture, took careful aim with his laser rifle, and fired.

Kzzzaakkk!

"Take that, tinhead!" Hikaru yelled. His

shot severed the cable that fed energy from the Fire Vulture's power source into the battle machine. The robot battle machine was now powerless.

Hikaru would have liked to capture the Fire Vulture and bring it back to base, but he knew other robots would be on their way. Just before the Fire Vulture spun out of the clouds and fell into the gorge below, Hikaru engaged the locator beacon on the robot battle machine's armor.

"That should throw the rest of the robots off track," Hikaru said. He knew the robot pilot would eject safely, but the beacon would draw all of the robot reinforcements to the gorge.

Hikaru set a course for the EXO-FORCE team's headquarters and flew off. He was relieved to have won, but one thing still bothered him.

That maneuver the Fire Vulture did — the veer, dive, and spin, he thought. *I've never seen a robot pilot do that. In* fact, I've only seen that maneuver done by one flier, long before there was an EXO-FORCE pilot. But he wouldn't have taught it to the robots ... would he? Troubled, Hikaru headed for home base to find some answers.

テクニカル
データ
ファイル

CHAPTER 2

After leaving the Stealth Hunter to be repaired and making his report to Keiken, Hikaru went for a walk through the base. He had not told Keiken about the Fire Vulture's aerial maneuvers, even though he knew he should have. He wanted to find out more before saying anything.

On his way to the tactical center, he saw his best friend, Takeshi. Pilot of the Grand Titan, the most powerful battle machine in the EXO-FORCE team, Takeshi was always training and trying to find ways to improve his skills. He hated the robots more than any other team member, and for good reason. His family — his father, Yukio, his mother, Akina, and his baby sister, Tamika — had been trapped on the south

side of the mountain when the robots had attacked. Takeshi had tried to save them, but it was too late. He had no idea what had become of them.

"What happened up there?" Takeshi asked. "I heard the Stealth Hunter was badly damaged."

"Fire Vulture," Hikaru answered. "The Sensei thinks it was scouting the base for an attack. He's putting the EXO-FORCE team on yellow alert."

"I hope they do attack," Takeshi said grimly. "I hope every robot over there comes across the bridges, so I can turn them into scrap metal."

Hikaru frowned. He had seen Takeshi

in battle. The Grand Titan was an amazing machine, but it wasn't indestructible. Yet Takeshi took all sorts of terrible risks in a fight, almost as if he were trying to defeat the robot army all by himself. Hikaru was sure it was because of Takeshi's family. He worried that one day Takeshi would take one risk too many.

"You should get some rest, Takeshi," said Hikaru. "If the robots do attack, we'll all need to be at our best."

"I have to keep training," Takeshi said, turning away. "I'll never let the EXO-FORCE team lose a battle because I wasn't ready."

Hikaru said good-bye to his friend and headed for the computer center. Here EXO-FORCE members could learn all about their battle machines, the robots' battle machines, and even the history of Sentai Mountain. It was history Hikaru was interested in today.

It didn't take him long to find what

he was looking for. Before the first robot rebellion, some engineers had begun experimenting with armored devices that could be worn by humans and piloted just like a vehicle. After much trial and error, these would eventually become the battle machines the EXO-FORCE team used today. In those days, one of the most skilled pilots was Takeshi's father, Yukio.

Hikaru watched vid-tapes of Yukio as a pilot. There it was — the very same maneuver the Fire Vulture had used. Yukio had invented that maneuver and used it all the time. If a robot pilot were using it, then the robot would have had to learn it from Yukio.

That means Takeshi's father

is still alive, Hikaru thought. *But is he a prisoner of the robots, or is he a traitor?*

There was only one way to find out. Hikaru would have to go to the south side of the mountain and rescue Yukio, his wife, and his daughter. No EXO-FORCE member had ever tried anything like that before. No one knew what defenses the robots might have in place.

But I have to do it, he told himself. *For Takeshi's sake . . . for the sake of his mother and sister . . . and for Yukio, no matter what he is doing.*

"What are you studying, Hikaru?"

Hikaru quickly switched the screen off and turned around. Ryo had come into the room. As always, he had a big smile on his face. The inventor was another of Hikaru's friends.

"I'm studying, um, great pilots of the past," Hikaru said. "I thought I might learn some new tricks."

"Well, if you do, you can try them out soon," Ryo said. "Uplink and I have finished fixing the Stealth Hunter. Next time, fly a little faster, okay?"

Hikaru smiled. Uplink was the name of Ryo's battle machine, a specially designed piece of equipment that could not only fight, but also repair other battle machines. For some reason, Ryo always talked about it as if it were a living person and not just metal and circuits.

"Hey, Ryo, what do you think is on the other side of the mountain?" Hikaru asked. "Do you think the robots have defenses there we can't overcome?"

"Give me enough tools and materials and I can build a battle machine that can overcome any-thing," Ryo said proudly. "But the robots are smart, too. Whenever we build a better battle machine, they build something even more powerful. Sometimes I wonder if this race to create more destructive weapons will ever stop."

Hikaru nodded. There was one other person he needed to talk to before he started this mission, even though he knew just what that person would say.

光　　光　　光

"No! Absolutely not!"

Sensei Keiken was angrier than Hikaru had ever seen him. The aged leader of the EXO-FORCE team was responsible for maintaining the security of the human side of the mountain, as well as recruiting and training new pilots. He could be stern, but it was only because he cared so much about the men and women under his command.

"But, Sensei —"

"No, Hikaru. We can't afford to risk you or the Stealth Hunter on an impossible

mission. You would need a full strike force to get into the robot camp, and even then I am not sure you could do it."

Keiken's expression changed to one of understanding. "Someday, we will be able to rescue all the humans trapped by the robots. Right now, we have to worry about stopping the robots from conquering any more of the mountain. Do you understand?"

"Saving all the humans starts with saving one," Hikaru answered. "Takeshi has saved my life more times than I can count. I owe it to him to do this."

Keiken shook his head. "You are to stay here, Hikaru. That's a direct order. Disobey and you will be out of the EXO-FORCE team."

Hikaru nodded and left the chamber. He loved being part of the EXO-FORCE team, doing his best to defend the mountain and flying through the sky in the Stealth Hunter. But if he had to lose all that in order to save Takeshi's family, it was just the chance he had to take.

This might be the last time I ever fly the Stealth Hunter, Hikaru thought as he headed through the EXO-FORCE headquarters to the hangar. Hikaru took a deep breath. *I better make it a good one.*

CHAPTER 3

Hikaru climbed into the Stealth Hunter battle machine a few hours before dawn. No one had questioned his coming for it so early — he was due to go on patrol now anyway. He just hadn't told anyone where he would really be going.

"Time to power up!" he said, hitting the controls. Energy flooded the battle machine, bringing it completely online in half a second. He checked the status of the weapons, the boot jets, the armor, the sensors, and the communications equipment. All were working well. Then he scanned the stealth technology built into the battle machine, making sure it was online and ready to go. Satisfied, he pressed a button on the wall that opened the hangar doors.

"Good luck!" Ryo shouted as Hikaru piloted the Stealth Hunter out into the darkness.

"Thanks," Hikaru replied. "I think I'm going to need it."

Standard procedure when piloting the Stealth Hunter was to put it into full stealth mode only in battle or when doing a recon mission over the robots' side of the mountain. The power needed to make the battle machine invisible to sensors was a huge energy drain. That was one of the risks of this mission. Even if he found Yukio and the others, he might not have the power left to fly them back to safety.

Still, there was no other choice. Just a minute after he left base, Hikaru turned on the stealth mode. He knew that Ryo would be going crazy back at base when he saw the Stealth Hunter disappear from the sensor screens. It felt strange to be hiding from his friends, but it was too late to turn back now.

He flew low over Tenchi Bridge, one of the many wide spans that linked the two sides of the mountain. Some on the human side believed the bridges should be destroyed to keep the robots from launching attacks over them. But Sensei Keiken had decided against that. Wrecking all the bridges would make it almost impossible for the humans ever to return to the other side of the mountain and save those still being held prisoner. No, the bridges would stand and it would be the EXO-FORCE team's job to defend them.

And it looks like it's time to go to work, he thought sadly as he flew over the southern peak. Down below, he could see two R-1 Robot Rammer vehicles and a half dozen Sentry battle machines winding along a

mountain road. They were headed for Tenchi Bridge. *They must be planning an attack on the EXO-FORCE base,* Hikaru thought.

Hikaru had to think fast. If he transmitted a warning back to base, his rescue mission would be over before it started. But he couldn't allow the robots to make a surprise attack.

There was only one chance. He switched off stealth mode for an instant and aimed and fired his laser rifle twice. *Kzzzaakk! Kzzaakkk!* Both beams hit their targets — the engines of the R-1 Rammers. The robot crews jumped to safety as their vehicles exploded. The wreckage would now act as a roadblock to the robots' march.

By the time they finish pushing that junk out of the way, it will be daylight, he thought, as he returned his battle machine to stealth mode. *Those rust buckets will never make it across the bridge by day without being spotted long before.*

As he went back to his original course,

Hikaru hoped his actions had not doomed his own mission.

光　　光　　光

"I had him for a second," Ryo said to the Sensei. "He appeared on the screen on the other side of Tenchi Bridge, shot up a few R-1 Rammers, then disappeared again."

Sensei Keiken frowned. Hikaru's patrol route didn't extend that far over to the robots' side of the mountain. What was he doing there? Was he trying to carry out that crazy mission of his?

"Put the base on red alert!" he ordered. "I want all laser cannons manned, and double the number of Gate Defenders in case the robots are planning an attack."

"Yes, Sensei," Ryo replied. "Sir, can you tell me what is going on? What is Hikaru doing?"

"I'm not sure," the Sensei answered. "But before this day is over, he will be remembered either as the greatest hero in the history of the EXO-FORCE team . . . or the greatest failure."

光　　光　　光

A brown-armored Iron Drone robot turned away from its monitor screen. It looked directly at the golden robot that sat in the center of the chamber.

"Scheduled Tenchi Bridge attack terminated," it reported. "Scanners reveal presence of Stealth Hunter."

"Where?" said the golden robot. Its name

was Meca One and it was the leader of the robots.

"It has vanished from our screens again," said the Iron Drone. "But it's projected course would bring it to this sector."

Meca One rose and looked at the scanner. According to the course the Iron Drone had plotted, the Stealth Hunter was heading for the research facility. If it were possible for a robot to smile, it would have done so. "We have gained much technical knowledge from our prisoners," it said. "But we could learn even more from examining a Stealth Hunter battle machine. It must be captured, along with its pilot. We will force both to surrender their secrets!"

CHAPTER 4

Hikaru flew as quickly as he could, keeping one eye on his surroundings and the other on his sensor screens. He had programmed the sensors with all the information available on Yukio, including his height, weight, voice pattern, and brain scan. If Takeshi's father were there, the sensors would find him.

So far, what Hikaru had seen on the ground below sickened him. All of the houses and farms that had once dotted this side of the mountain had been torn down and replaced with factories that filled the sky with dark smoke. He could see human workers going into the mines, but without any protective gear on.

Those mines weren't built for humans, thought Hikaru. *They were designed for robot workers, who couldn't be hurt so eas-*

ily. If they are making the prisoners do this dangerous work, who knows what else they are making them do?

Hikaru flew on. His battle machine's vid-recorders were on so he could capture everything he saw and show it to Sensei Keiken later. He flew over a repair yard where damaged Fire Vultures and Thunder Furies were being welded back together. He saw the huge doors of a hangar open and a newly constructed Sonic Phantom aircraft roll out. In the center of the compound, Iron Drones in their Sentry battle machines and R-1 Robot Rammers practiced a gate assault.

But what most caught Hikaru's attention was a large, square metal building perched high on the mountain slope. It was ringed with Iron Drones, and two Thunder Furies patrolled the gates. If the robots wanted to keep whatever was inside safe, they had picked the perfect spot. To reach this building, the human forces would first have to fight their way across one of the many bridges that connected the two sides of the mountain and then cross the entire robot compound.

Hikaru's thoughts were interrupted when the Stealth Hunter's sensor screen lit up. Yukio was somewhere inside that building!

Hikaru decided not to take any chances.

To make sure the robots would not hear him coming, he cut off his boot jets and glided toward the building. On the way down, Hikaru was reminded of something he had done as a little boy. One afternoon, he thought it would be fun to play with a hornet's nest. When he poked the nest with a stick, the angry insects swarmed out and stung him so many times he had to go to the hospital.

And now I am about to upset another nest — but this one's filled with a much more dangerous creature, he thought. *Let's hope history doesn't repeat itself.*

The building was well protected, but Hikaru saw one weakness. The robots had not prepared for an aerial attack. The robots must have thought that their Sonic Phantom and Fire Vultures would stop any invaders before they got this close.

Hikaru turned on his boot jets at the last moment so he could make a soft landing on the roof. He waited a moment before doing anything else. He wanted to be completely sure no robots had detected his arrival. Even though his stealth technology was still activated, he didn't  want to take any foolish chances.

What am I saying? he thought. *This whole mission is foolish!*

He moved the Stealth Hunter carefully across the rooftop until his sensors showed Yukio was alone in the room right beneath him. He set his electro-sword on low intensity and used it to cut a hole in the roof. Using a mini tractor beam, he caught the piece of roof before it could fall and set it aside. Then he dropped into the building.

Immediately, Yukio spun around. "Who is there?"

Through the cockpit window, Hikaru saw Yukio in what appeared to be a laboratory. Yukio was wearing a white lab coat and studying a damaged battle machine.

"Sssshhhh!" whispered Hikaru through his suit microphone. "Keep quiet! I'm in stealth mode. I'm here to rescue you."

"No!" said Yukio. "This is another robot trick!"

"Yukio, it's Hikaru. Trust me. Is there

any way you can block this room off from the robots' sensors?"

The scientist nodded, still not completely convinced. "Yes. One of my repair devices causes interference. The robots won't be able to scan while it is running."

"Turn it on," said Hikaru.

Yukio switched on the device, which made a loud hum. As soon as it was active, Hikaru switched off his stealth technology. The Stealth Hunter, with Hikaru inside, suddenly became visible. Yukio jumped at the sudden appearance of his son's friend.

"Hikaru? Is that really you?" he asked, peering into the cockpit. "Is Takeshi with you?"

"No," replied Hikaru. "But I am going to bring you, your wife, and your daughter to him."

Yukio shook his head. "It's impossible. There are too many guards, too many battle machines. You'll never make it. I don't know how you got here, but you must go back before it is too late!"

"You're right. It is impossible," Hikaru said, smiling. "That's what makes it worth doing."

He glanced around. There were all sorts of devices and battle machine parts scattered around the lab. "Yukio, before we leave, I have to ask you one thing," he said. "I saw a Fire Vulture do a maneuver in the air that only you would know how to do. Have you . . . have you been helping the robots? Please tell me you aren't working for those junk heaps!"

Yukio's face filled with anger. "I didn't have a choice! The robots hooked me up to a cerebro-scanner and stole top-secret information from me. I would never betray my home or my people!"

"Why would the robots need to do that?" asked Hikaru. "They have computer minds — much faster than ours, and maybe even smarter, too."

"But they have no imagination," Yukio said. "No creativity. They cannot come up with anything new. All they can do is rebuild their old battle machines and try to make them better. Every new device they have created — the Sonic Phantom, the Raging Storm — all of those were based on my ideas."

"Well, they won't be able steal from you anymore!" said Hikaru. "Where is your family?"

Yukio told him that his wife, Akina, and his daughter, Tamika, were just down the hall in the living quarters. "But we can't go out the laboratory door. As soon as we open it, an alarm will sound!"

"Who says we're going out the door?" Hikaru answered with a smirk as he triggered his electro-sword. Sensors told him there were no robots on the other side of the wall. With two swift strokes, he carved a hole in the wall that led to the corridor. Just as he had done before, he carefully pulled the loose piece into the lab and set it down on the floor. Reactivating his battle machine's stealth mode, he piloted the Stealth Hunter through the hole.

Strange, he thought. *No alarms, no sirens, no explosions. I'd have thought the robots would have this place wired against any intruders. What's going on here?*

There was no time to think about it now. The Stealth Hunter's sensors picked up two human readings from the room at the end of the hall — Akina and Tamika. A single Sentry guarded the room. Hikaru indicated that Yukio should stay in the shadows while he maneuvered the invisible Stealth Hunter a bit closer. He took aim with his laser rifle and fired.

Kzzaakk! The shot was right on target. It struck a joint in the Sentry armor and hit the control circuits inside, fusing the battle machine so it could not move.

Shooom! The Sentry still managed to fire a missile at the Stealth Hunter.

Hikaru frantically tried to remember what Ryo had taught him about blocking robot missiles. Sonics, that was it! The right sound broadcast over the Stealth Hunter's radio could jam a Sentry missile.

Turning up his radio to full volume, he triggered a high-pitched whine over the speakers. The missile wavered in its flight, then turned straight up and blasted through the ceiling. Hikaru looked up in time to see it explode high in the sky.

Well, if the metal monsters didn't know I was here before, they know now, he said to himself. *Better move fast!*

Hikaru disabled the Sentry's weapons systems with two quick laser rifle shots. *He won't cause us any more trouble,* Hikaru thought. He used the Stealth Hunter's right arm to knock the locked door off its hinges. Yukio rushed in to reassure his wife and daughter everything was all right.

"Yukio!" cried Akina. "I was so afraid. I thought it was the robots coming for us!"

"They'll never threaten you again," Yukio replied. "Hikaru's going to help us. We will be free soon."

"I wish!" said Hikaru. "We still have to get out of here — and it won't be easy. You three will have to hang on to the outside of the Stealth Hunter. I can't use the stealth technology — it drains too much power, and combined with your weight, it will slow down our flight. I'll just have to outfly everything on the base!"

Yukio and his family followed the Stealth Hunter back out into the corridor. They stopped below the hole blown in the roof by the Sentry missile. Alarms were sounding all over the base. Fire Vultures could be seen circling above, waiting for their prey to emerge.

"Grab hold of the battle machine and don't let go!" Hikaru triggered the battle machine's boot jets, but right away he could see that the weight of three extra

passengers was going to slow the Stealth Hunter way down.

As soon as he piloted the Stealth Hunter back up through the roof, Hikaru was reminded of that nest of angry hornets again. Robots were everywhere!

Hikaru ran a quick scan of the building he had just left. There were no humans or robots left inside. Hikaru located the electro-furnace in the center of the building with his sensors, fired a laser bolt, and then pushed his speed to the maximum.

Ka-whammm! The building exploded, sending fire and smoke high into the air and knocking the Fire Vultures off course.

"What's the matter, canheads?" Hikaru asked. "Didn't learn 'flying through big explosions' at robot school?"

Now the entire base was alive with activity. A hail of laser fire erupted from the ground, forcing the Stealth Hunter to fly in a zigzag pattern to avoid being hit. More Fire Vultures were rocketing up in pursuit, their flamethrowers hurling jets of fire.

Worst of all, a Sonic Phantom had taken off and was closing in fast on the Stealth Hunter. The powerful aircraft was one of the most frightening weapons in the robot army.

"I have to turn and fight it, there's no other way," Hikaru broadcast to Yukio through the battle machine's speakers. "I am going to leave you and your family on a ridge. You'll be safe there for now."

"No," said Akina. "You mustn't sacrifice yourself for us. Just leave us and go before they capture you!"

"Wait!" said Yukio. "The Sonic Phantom was built from ideas they stole from me. I know how you can defeat it!"

"Then talk fast!" said Hikaru. "We don't have much time!"

CHAPTER 5

A burst of speed bought Hikaru enough time to drop Yukio and his family to temporary safety on the ridge. Now it was time to face the Sonic Phantom.

He had fought the Sonic Phantom several times before and barely managed to survive. Once, he had even been able to disable a Phantom, but that was when the Stealth Hunter was at full power. There was no way the Stealth Hunter could do that again after spending all this time in full stealth mode. The battle machine's power was dangerously low.

By this time, the Sonic Phantom had outpaced the Fire Vultures and was getting ready to fire missiles. The robot pilot expected the Stealth Hunter to evade, but Hikaru had another idea, thanks to Yukio. He transferred all power into his boot jets and rocketed straight for the Sonic Phantom.

The Sonic Phantom fired its laser cannons. One blast badly damaged the Stealth Hunter's right arm. A collision alarm went off on Hikaru's control console. Still, he kept flying right for the Sonic Phantom. One of

them was going to have to turn or there would be a crash.

Yukio's idea might just work! Hikaru thought. He knew robots always reacted with logic. Sometimes that was a great strength, but other times it was a weakness. Knowing how few Sonic Phantoms there were and how hard it was to build them, the robot pilot would never risk destroying one in a collision with the Stealth Hunter. Just an instant before the crash, the robot pilot pulled back the control stick, sending the nose of the Sonic Phantom up into the air. Yukio's plan had worked!

This was Hikaru's chance. The weaker underside of the Sonic Phantom was exposed as it tried to gain altitude. Hikaru charged up the Stealth Hunter's electro-sword. At his command, the Stealth Hunter's arm swung the sword and sliced open the bottom of the Sonic Phantom. Sparks flew and smoke began to billow from the tear in the metal.

"Now for the real trick," Hikaru said. He made the Stealth Hunter's mechanical hand grab hold of the hole he had torn in the Sonic Phantom's armor. The robot pilot was flying loops, trying to shake him off, but the Stealth Hunter hung on. As dangerous as this stunt was, it was the safest place the Stealth Hunter could have been. In this position, the Sonic Phantom could not fire missiles at him without blowing itself up, and the Fire Vultures wouldn't take the chance of torching their own aircraft.

Hikaru reached in with the Stealth Hunter's free hand and found the wires he was looking for. One was red, one was green, and one was blue — just as Yukio had said. Each controlled a part of the ship's navigation system, but if they were fused together . . .

That's when the fun starts, Hikaru thought.

He released an electric current through his battle machine's hand and melted the three wires together. Then he began sending electrical pulses into the fused wires. The Sonic Phantom suddenly changed course, heading back for base.

I did it! Hikaru thought. *I've taken control of the Sonic Phantom!*

It wouldn't last long, he knew. The robot pilot would soon find a way to bypass what he had done. But it was long enough to

finish his plan. He increased the Sonic Phantom's speed and aimed it right at the oncoming Fire Vultures.

The Fire Vulture pilots didn't see the danger in time. Hikaru released his grip on the Sonic Phantom just before it crashed into the Fire Vultures. Spiraling out of control, the Sonic Phantom and the Fire Vultures plummeted toward the ground.

"That's one Phantom they won't be able to fix," Hikaru said as he turned the Stealth

Hunter around to pick up Yukio and his family.

光　　　光　　　光

Ryo and the Sensei had been nervously watching the monitor screen ever since the Stealth Hunter's battle with the R-1 Rammers. The Sensei had told no one else that Hikaru had left the base and headed for the robot side of the mountain. If the other EXO-FORCE pilots knew, they would insist on going to help him and might fly right into a trap.

Suddenly, Ryo pointed to a flying figure on the screen. "He's coming back!"

"Maintain red alert in case he has robots pursuing him," Sensei Keiken ordered. Then he managed a little smile, relieved that Hikaru was safe. "And tell Takeshi to man the gate."

The gunner on the Tenchi Bridge gate couldn't believe his eyes when he saw the Stealth Hunter approaching. He blinked

his eyes to make sure he wasn't seeing things. No, the Stealth Hunter was carrying humans!

From up above, Hikaru spotted Takeshi in the Grand Titan battle machine. He cut back his speed so he could give his passengers a soft landing. The Stealth Hunter landed right in front of the Grand Titan.

At first, Takeshi seemed angry. Where

had Hikaru been? How could he just take off like that? Then he saw who the Stealth Hunter had been carrying. He smiled and tears filled his eyes. Takeshi looked back to see the Sensei approaching. The Sensei gave the "all clear" signal, meaning it was all right for the pilots to leave their battle machines. Takeshi leaped out of the Grand Titan to hug his father, mother, and sister.

"You disobeyed orders," said the Sensei to Hikaru.

"I know, sir," Hikaru replied. "And I am ready to accept any punishment."

The Sensei shook his head. "But what punishment fits this crime? You invaded the robot side of the mountain, and even though you managed to escape with Takeshi's family, you took a serious risk. No, the only thing we can do is take the Stealth Hunter away from you."

Hikaru did his best not to look as upset as he felt. "Yes, Sensei."

"After all," said the Sensei, smiling, "you cannot fly two battle machines at once."

Hikaru looked at him, surprised. Then he saw Ryo emerging from the hangar with a powerful, blue-armored battle machine. It was the most amazing thing Hikaru had ever seen. It had sleek, powerful light-blue armor that would allow it to practically disappear against the sky. Hikaru could only imagine what new weapons it might have or how fast it would fly.

"Meet the Silent Strike," said the Sensei. "It's yours now, Hikaru. Fly it with honor."

Hikaru didn't know what to say. But when he turned and saw his best friend in the arms of his family, he knew that just maybe there were times when words were not needed.